This book belongs to

. . . .

Front endpapers by Amber Parker aged 7
Back endpapers by Maggie Thomas aged 7
Thank you to Star of the Sea RC Primary School, Whitley Bay
for helping with the endpapers – K.P.

For Margaret Shewan, to celebrate her 70th birthday – V.T.
For Helen Mortimer – K.P.

OXFORD
UNIVERSITY PRESS

Great Clarendon Street, Oxford OX2 6DP

Oxford University Press is a department of the University of Oxford.
It furthers the University's objective of excellence in research, scholarship,
and education by publishing worldwide in

Oxford New York

Auckland Cape Town Dar es Salaam Hong Kong Karachi
Kuala Lumpur Madrid Melbourne Mexico City Nairobi
New Delhi Shanghai Taipei Toronto

With offices in

Argentina Austria Brazil Chile Czech Republic France Greece
Guatemala Hungary Italy Japan Poland Portugal Singapore
South Korea Switzerland Thailand Turkey Ukraine Vietnam

Oxford is a registered trade mark of Oxford University Press
in the UK and in certain other countries

British Library Cataloguing in Publication Data available

ISBN: 978-0-19-272909-5 (paperback)

ISBN: 978-0-19-272910-1 (paperback with audio CD)

Printed in Singapore

Paper used in the production of this book is a natural, recyclable product made
from wood grown in sustainable forests. The manufacturing process conforms to the
environmental regulations of the country of origin

Valerie Thomas and Korky Paul

Winnie's
Amazing Pumpkin

OXFORD

UNIVERSITY PRESS

Winnie the Witch ate lots of vegetables.

She liked broccoli, cauliflower,
cabbage, and parsnips.
She really liked peas, carrots,
beans, potatoes, and spinach.

But she *loved* pumpkin.
She loved pumpkin soup, pumpkin pie, and
pumpkin scones with pumpkin seeds on top.
But, most of all, she loved roast pumpkin.

Wilbur, her big black cat,
liked pumpkin soup if it
had lots of cream stirred in.

Every Saturday morning Winnie
would jump onto her broomstick,
Wilbur would jump onto her
shoulder, and they would zoom
off to the farmers' market
to buy their vegetables.

That was easy.

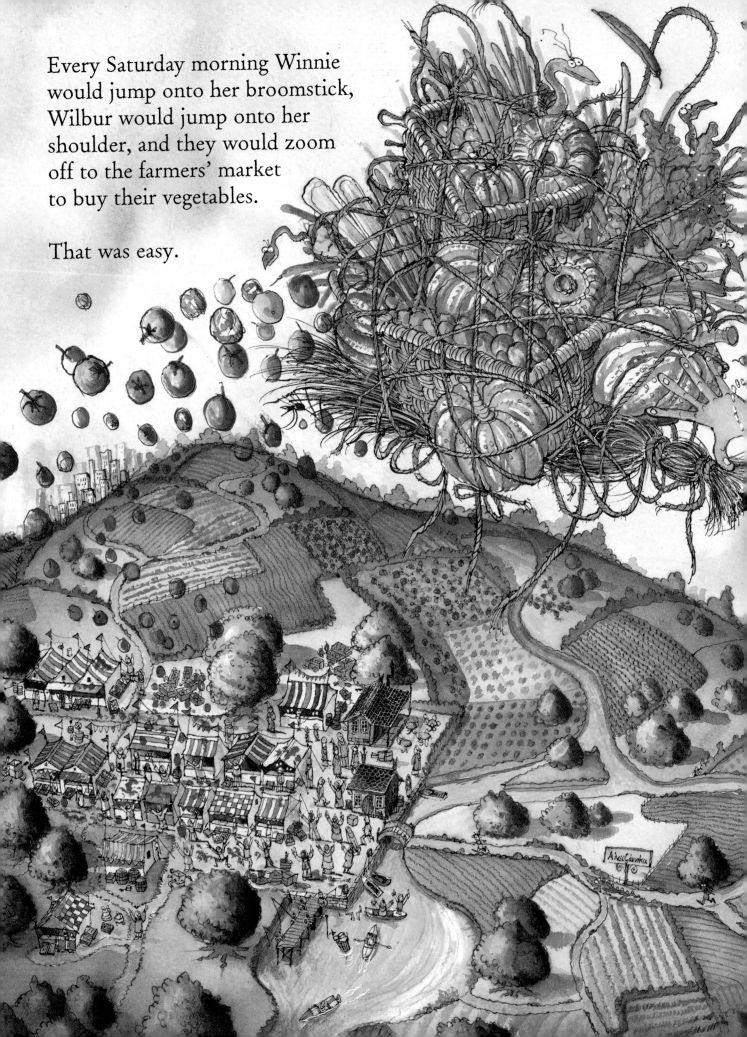

But it wasn't so easy coming home.
It is hard to balance on a broomstick with
a cat, pumpkins, and lots of other vegetables.

Ooops! Brussels sprouts and tomatoes
rained down on the market.

Splat! Squelch!

'Blithering broomsticks!' shouted Winnie.
And then she had a good idea.

'I'll grow my own vegetables,' she said.
So Winnie dug a big vegetable patch
in her garden.

Wilbur helped.

She planted lots and lots of vegetables.
She watered the plants and pulled up
the weeds.

Wilbur helped.

But the plants grew very slowly.

And, when they did grow, the caterpillars and snails and rabbits ate them.

'Oh dear,' said Winnie. 'Gardening is hard work. I'll try a spell to help my garden grow.'

She waved her magic wand, shouted,

Abracadabra!

and nothing happened.

'Bother!' said Winnie.
'That didn't work.
I'll go and look in my
Big Book of Spells.'

Winnie went inside
just a minute too soon.

Outside, the spell
began to work.

Inside, it was very dark.
Winnie tripped over Wilbur.

'Meooowww!'

'I'm sorry, Wilbur,' said Winnie,
'I didn't see you. It's so dark, there
must be a storm on the way.'

She looked out of the window.
It wasn't a storm.
It was Winnie's garden.
The vegetables were growing so fast
they covered all the windows.

'I'd better go out and stop
the spell,' Winnie said.

But the door wouldn't open.
An enormous cabbage was in the way.

Winnie rushed upstairs, climbed
out of the bathroom window,
and slid down a giant beanstalk.

Wilbur climbed down behind her.
'This is fun!' he thought,
until he met a giant caterpillar.
'Yeeoow!'

Everything in Winnie's garden was
enormous, gigantic, stupendous!

A beanstalk was growing up into the clouds.
The cabbages were as big as cows.
The rabbits were bigger than cows.
An immense pumpkin vine was curling
around Winnie's house.

And there, on the roof, was a **huge** pumpkin.
'Oh no!' shouted Winnie.
'The pumpkin will squash my house!'
She waved her magic wand,
but just as she shouted . . .

Abra . . .

CRASH!

. . . cadabra!

the gigantic pumpkin
crashed to the ground.

Winnie's enormous, stupendous garden
shrank back to the way it was before.

But the pumpkin that had broken
off the vine was still a massive,
monstrous, amazing pumpkin.

Winnie chopped a doorway into the pumpkin.

She made pumpkin pies, pumpkin scones,
pumpkin soup with cream for Wilbur, and
an enormous dish of roast pumpkin.

But there was still lots of pumpkin left.

So she put a notice on the gate:

☆FREE☆ PUMPKIN ☆
Help yourself...

People came with their bowls and baskets and even wheelbarrows.

And soon the pumpkin shell was empty.

'What shall I do with the pumpkin shell?' wondered Winnie.
'It would make a good house, but I already have a house.

One of my friends once changed a pumpkin into a coach.
But that was for a special occasion.
And the horses might be a problem.'

Then Winnie had a wonderful idea.
'Yes!' she said. 'That's exactly what
it looks like,' she said. 'Of course!'

She waved her magic wand,
stamped her foot, shouted,

Abracadabra!

and there, in Winnie's garden,
was a bright orange helicopter.

So now, when Winnie and Wilbur go to the market, Winnie can buy as many pumpkins as she likes.

And flying home in a helicopter is lots of fun!

Winnie's Pumpkin Soup

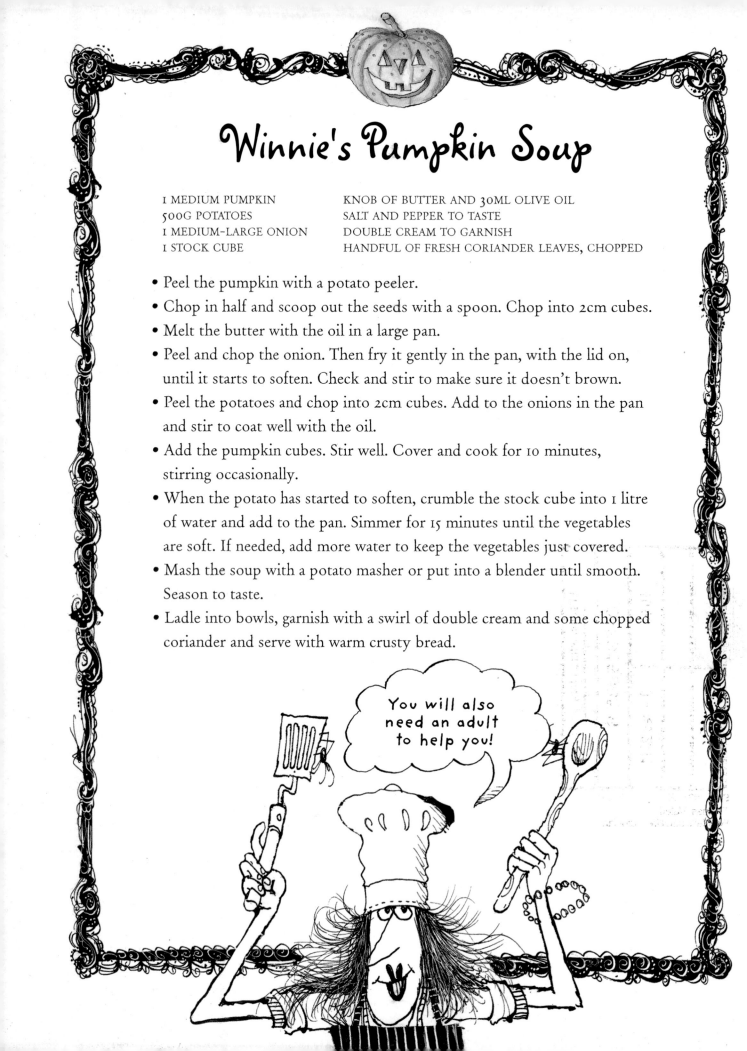

1 MEDIUM PUMPKIN
500G POTATOES
1 MEDIUM-LARGE ONION
1 STOCK CUBE

KNOB OF BUTTER AND 30ML OLIVE OIL
SALT AND PEPPER TO TASTE
DOUBLE CREAM TO GARNISH
HANDFUL OF FRESH CORIANDER LEAVES, CHOPPED

- Peel the pumpkin with a potato peeler.
- Chop in half and scoop out the seeds with a spoon. Chop into 2cm cubes.
- Melt the butter with the oil in a large pan.
- Peel and chop the onion. Then fry it gently in the pan, with the lid on, until it starts to soften. Check and stir to make sure it doesn't brown.
- Peel the potatoes and chop into 2cm cubes. Add to the onions in the pan and stir to coat well with the oil.
- Add the pumpkin cubes. Stir well. Cover and cook for 10 minutes, stirring occasionally.
- When the potato has started to soften, crumble the stock cube into 1 litre of water and add to the pan. Simmer for 15 minutes until the vegetables are soft. If needed, add more water to keep the vegetables just covered.
- Mash the soup with a potato masher or put into a blender until smooth. Season to taste.
- Ladle into bowls, garnish with a swirl of double cream and some chopped coriander and serve with warm crusty bread.

You will also need an adult to help you!